Five Little Seals

Written by Kristin Yook
Illustrated by Sadie Peers

IMAGINEWE
Publishers™

ImagineWe Publishers
A Global Publisher

Published by ImagineWe, LLC
ImagineWe Publishers
247 Market Street, Suite 201
Lockport, NY 14094
United States
www.imaginewepublishers.com

© 2023 ImagineWe, LLC

ISBN: 978-1-946512-73-4
Library of Congress Control Number: 2023904225

First Edition

We are always looking for new authors. For more information, please visit the website liste above. To shop our selection of books and merchandise you can visit:
www.shop.imaginewepublishers.com

To Sabrina and Richard, you are my world and always my why!
To my husband I couldn't do this thing
called life without you by my side.

I love you my family more than words could ever express.

To my Sprouts & Friends families, thank you from the bottom
of my heart for allowing me to create joy with you and your
sprouting little ones. Are you ready to play?

Five little seals went out one day.

Over the waves and far away.

But only four little seals came back.

Four little seals went out one day.

Over the waves and far away.

But only three little seals came back.

Three little seals went out one day.

Over the waves and far away.

Mama seal barked
errp, errp, errp, errp...

But only two little seals came back.

Two little seals went out one day.

Over the waves and far away.

Mama seal barked
errp, errp, errp, errp...

But only one little seal came back.

One little seal went out one day.

Over the waves and far away.

But none of the five
little seals came back.

Sad Mama seal went out one day.

Over the waves and far away.

And all of the five little seals came back.

Kristin Yook

Kristin Yook was born in 1981 and raised in Brooklyn, NY. She received her B.A. in Psychology and Philosophy from SUNY Binghamton as well as an M.A. in School Psychology at Adelphi University. She worked as a School Psychologist and served as the Program Director for a non-profit organization teaching Parent Education before starting her own family. After becoming a mother, she dedicated 10 years to raising her children before opening her own music and movement business for families with children from birth through age five called Sprouts & Friends, Inc. She currently resides on Long Island, NY with her husband and two children.

Made in the USA
Middletown, DE
22 April 2023

29114954R00018